VAMPIRE BOY'S GOOD NIGHT

LISA BROWN

HARPER
An Imprint of HarperCollinsPublishers

Vampire Boy's Good Night
Copyright © 2010 by Lisa Brown
All rights reserved.
Manufactured in China.
No part of this book may be used or
reproduced in any manner whatsoever
without written permission except in the case
of brief quotations embodied in critical articles
and reviews. For information address
HarperCollins Children's Books, a division of
HarperCollins Publishers, 10 East 53rd Street,
New York, NY 10022.
www.harpercollinschildrens.com

Library of Congress
catalog card number: 2009023549
ISBN 978-0-06-114044-2 (trade bdg.)

Book design by
Alison Donalty & Torborg Davern
10 11 12 13 14   LEO   10 9 8 7 6 5 4 3 2 1
❖ First Edition

TO DANIEL ♡

When the sun goes down and everything is wonderfully cold and dark . . .

the vampire boy wakes
up thirsty for breakfast.

He pulls on his gloves.
He fastens his cape.

CAW.

MORGAN

He sets out into the night to pay a visit.

"I'm almost ready,"
says the little witch.
"Just let me finish
my brew."
Morgan takes a sip.

She buckles her shoes.
She puts on her hat.

PAGANINI

Danse
Macabre
Saint-Saëns

Symphonie
Fantastique
BERLIOZ

BABOON
BLOOD

Bela and Morgan climb on a broomstick
and fly out the window.

"What shall we do tonight?" asks Morgan.
"I want to look for children," says Bela. "I want to see their rosy cheeks and their tiny white teeth."
"Silly Bela," says Morgan. "There are no such things."

WHOOO?

CHILDREN ARE NOT REAL!

"I've heard they like to swing and climb," says Bela,
but there is nobody in the park.
"They sit in rows and write in lines," says Bela,
but no one is at school.
"They play with bats," says Bela,
but the baseball fields are empty.
"See?" says Morgan. "Children don't really exist."

Far below they see lights.
"What's that?" asks Bela, pointing.

Bela and Morgan land on the lawn.
There are cobwebs on the porch and
jack-o'-lanterns on the stoop.
A skeleton hangs from the door.
"Come in, come in!" says a little ghoul.

WHAT A BEAUTIFUL HOUSE!

I'M IN ON A PLOT

EXCUSE MY DUST

BELOVED FATHER

CALLED BACK

"Are they children?" asks Bela.
"I don't know," says Morgan.
"Where are their rosy cheeks?
Where are their tiny white teeth?"

THEY LOOK JUST LIKE US!

Bela and Morgan join the party.
The ghouls bob for apples.
They tell scary stories.
They play pin the tail
on the cat.
"Now it's time for the
contest," says a ghost.

There are three ghosts,
two goblins,
and one pirate queen.

There's a monster,
a mummy, a cat,
and a clown.

Morgan is the only witch
who doesn't have warts.

"Look at that vampire," says the pirate.
"He is the scariest!"
But she isn't talking about Bela.

The party is coming to an end.
The ghouls take off their masks.
Underneath are pink cheeks and white teeth.
Bela and Morgan laugh with surprise and forget
their goody bags as they leave.

They find the broom in the bushes and fly into the dark.

"I *told* you that children are real," says Bela.
"Well, *you* should have won the contest,"
says Morgan.

Bela and Morgan weave in and out and
above the trees until the sun begins to rise.
Bela yawns. It is time to go home.

Bela is tired.
He gets in his bed
and folds up his hands.
He dreams about apples
and pirates.

Zzzzz

Sleep tight, vampire boy, until night falls again.

BELA